WINTER'S HEART

(A Heat of Love Holiday Bonus Story)

BY LETA BLAKE

An Original Publication from Leta Blake Books

Winter's Heart
Written and published by Leta Blake
Cover by Dar Albert
Formatted by BB eBooks

Other Books by Leta Blake

Contemporary

Will & Patrick Wake Up Married
Will & Patrick's Endless Honeymoon
Cowboy Seeks Husband
The Difference Between
Bring on Forever
Stay Lucky

Sports

The River Leith

The Training Season Series
Training Season
Training Complex

Musicians

Smoky Mountain Dreams
Vespertine

New Adult

Punching the V-Card

'90s Coming of Age Series
Pictures of You
You Are Not Me
Only You

Winter Holidays

North's Pole

The Mr. Christmas Series
Mr. Frosty Pants
Mr. Naughty List
Mr. Jingle Bells

A Boy for All Seasons
My December Daddy

Fantasy

Any Given Lifetime

Reimagined Fairy Tales

Flight
Levity

Paranormal & Shifters

Angel Undone
Omega Mine

Horror

Raise Up Heart

Omegaverse

Heat of Love Series
White Heat
Slow Heat
Alpha Heat
Slow Birth
Bitter Heat

For Sale Series
Heat for Sale
Bully for Sale

Audiobooks
letablake.com/audiobooks

Discover more about the author online

Leta Blake
letablake.com

Acknowledgements

Thank you to the following people: Mom and Dad, Brian and Cecily. All the wonderful members of my Patreon who inspire, support, and advise me. Keira Andrews for constant cheerleading. Devon Vesper for the amazing editing work. Dar Albert for the gorgeous cover. And thank you to my readers who make it all worthwhile.

About the Book

Winter-fox always brings Tristan the best gifts

Tristan wakes every winter holiday to find a present that delights him or teaches him an important lesson.

Learn more about the character of Tristan, *Bitter Heat's* Kerry and Janus's son, in this short winter holiday-themed story. This small bonus book doesn't contain the heat level of the full-length novels in this series, but it has all the cozy, hopeful warmth for a sweet holiday read. While it ends on a romantic note, the story does **not** contain a romance arc.

This story is **not a standalone** and is best read as an addition to the *Heat of Love* series, preferably after reading *Bitter Heat*. But if you should happen to read it out of order, you can find the rest of the books in the series here:

SLOW HEAT
ALPHA HEAT
BITTER HEAT
SLOW BIRTH
WINTER'S TRUTH
& series PREQUEL: WHITE HEAT

Dedication

Dedicated to my patrons at Patreon who support the business end of making books and audiobooks. Thank you to the fans of the *Heat of Love* universe! This bonus story is also for you!

CHAPTER ONE

"ONCE UPON A time, during the deep, dark months of the year, wolf-god's small brother, known as winter-fox, grew bored. The world was silent and blanketed in snow. No birds sang. No bears roamed—"

"Bears, Father?" Tristan asked from his perch on Janus's knee. His big, blue eyes were as wide as saucers, and he waved his wet thumb around having pulled it from his plump lips to ask. "What about the wildcats?"

Kerry, listening from his stuffed chair next to the sofa, lifted a brow. His knitting needles clicked as he waited for his *Érosgápe* mate's response. One long row of stitches turned into another. Tonight, just in time, he'd finish the blanket for Tristan's new bed.

Over on the sofa, Janus held the leather book open and blinked at the illustration. "I don't see any wildcats in this drawing."

Tristan sighed and squirmed a little. He'd had a fascination with the wildcats roaming their mountains ever since his close call with one the summer before. "But why not, Father? The wildcats don't sleep in winter. They like to wrestle. I've seen them. Why didn't winter-fox play with them if he was bored?"

Janus met Kerry's gaze and said, "Well, maybe he tried. Maybe the cats didn't like him."

"Why?"

Kerry chuckled. "Let your father finish the story. It's nearly bedtime."

The reminder of bedtime made Tristan's little eyebrows draw down in a frown. Still he was insistent. "But *why* didn't the cats like winter-fox, Pater? He's a jolly friend. He decorates the trees. He plays the winter bells so they echo in the hills. He gives wonderful presents." Tristan's wet thumb slashed through the air with each point. "I think they *should* like him."

"Well, it's a good thing they didn't," Kerry said. "Or winter-fox would never have been bored enough to dream up the Feast of Winter's Heart."

"We don't *eat* winter-fox's heart, do we?" Tristan asked in a whisper, leaning forward toward Kerry like he might climb out of his father's lap and over to his pater for comfort. "I don't want to eat his heart, Pater!"

"Of course not!" Janus reassured him, tugging him back firmly and kissing the top of his head. "The heart is figurative."

Tristan tilted his head. "Fig-tive?"

"It just means that the Feast takes place in the middle or the 'heart' of winter," Kerry said, his own heart tugging with Tristan's earnest goodness.

Tristan was so sweet with animals and so soft with other children. It warmed Kerry to the core seeing him with Janus's patients' infants. Tristan was incredibly gentle when he touched them, pressing sweet kisses to their heads and cheeks. Not a trace of cruel Monhundy blood showing through. Thank wolf-god.

Janus reassured their son. "Winter-fox's heart is safe."

"'Less he meets his *Érosgápe*," Tristan said solemnly. "Then his heart is lost for good. That's right, isn't it? That's what the stories say." He put a hand over his own chest. "I don't want to lose my heart."

Kerry snorted. He'd wondered whether his own pater had been reading to Tristan from the sappy romance novels he liked so well, and now he had his answer. "*Érosgápe* don't lose their heart. Put your hand on your father's chest. You'll feel his beating there, and you've heard mine when you rest your head on me."

Tristan narrowed his eyes and put his hand on Janus's chest. "What if it's your heart in there? What if you traded? I traded my peach for Adin's apple once. What if it's like that?"

Janus sighed and put aside the story.

Kerry smiled.

Tristan had heard the winter-fox tale several times before, but never with so many questions. Well, that wasn't true. In the past, the questions had been about the holiday—*"Is it true winter-fox will bring me gifts while I sleep?"*—and not about wildcats and traveling hearts.

Janus said, "*Érosgápe*—like your pater and I—share a love like no other, but we didn't swap hearts, and if you find your *Érosgápe*, your heart will stay in your chest, too. I promise."

Kerry wondered if that was a lie. Sometimes it felt as if his heart was cleaved in half and walked around outside his body in the shapes of Janus and Tristan, but he wasn't about to say that out loud. His sweet boy was already confused enough.

"Bedtime," Janus announced, heaving up to standing and steadying Tristan onto his own little feet. "Winter-fox comes tonight, and you have to be well asleep, or he'll pass us by."

Tristan's eyes widened, and he nodded solemnly. "I'll sleep. I promise. I'll sleep good."

After Tristan had kissed Kerry goodnight and Janus had taken the boy up to bed, Kerry shifted over to the sofa, before returning to his knitting. The room was warm, cozy protection against the snow falling just out the window. The fire twinkled merrily in the grate, as Kerry stretched his socked feet out beneath the blanket he was making. He continued his work while listening to the clomp of Janus's footsteps above and the little sounds of Tristan getting ready for sleep.

Peace had settled over him by the time

Janus returned, a wry grin on his face and a sweetness in his eye. "That boy asks me more questions than any of my teachers ever did."

"He's smart."

Janus lifted Kerry's feet and sat on the sofa, lowering them back into his lap. He rubbed the arches gently, and Kerry moaned with gratitude. "He's like his pater."

Kerry said nothing. Tristan *looked* more like a Monhundy—built big and strong, with fair skin and hair—but inside, he was different from that family through and through. The connection was something Kerry still struggled with from time to time when an innocent shift of Tristan's features revealed an expression too much like the alpha who'd made him. But, for the most part, as the years passed and Tristan flourished—good, wholesome, innocent— Kerry's old, traumatic associations faded, replaced by new, fiercely loving feelings.

Janus lifted Kerry's right foot and kissed the arch. "He's going to be very excited tomorrow morning."

"I hope so."

"It's his first Feast of Winter's Heart. Of course he'll be excited."

Kerry smiled. "It's been so many years since we celebrated Winter's Heart here. I was twelve when Pater gave it up."

"Well, surely you knew by then that winter-fox was just a story?"

"Of course." Kerry finished another row and began a fresh one. "I was proud that Pater thought I was old enough for the truth. I felt very mature. But now it seems a shame that it's only a holiday for children. There's so much fun in it."

"Presents, and decorations, and the winter bells…"

"I think the bells are his favorite part so far," Kerry said.

During the week leading up to the Feast of Winter's Heart, every night, after the sun fell, the mountains came alive with the sound of bells. This was the first year in ages that

Monk House had participated by ringing bells of their own. In the past, they'd simply sat back and listened to the bells rising all around them, a sound of joy in the dark, announcing that winter-fox was on his way. The children of the mountains grew more excited with each passing evening, making it nearly impossible to settle them in bed once the bells stopped ringing the final evening.

"What was the feast like for you, growing up in the city?" Kerry asked.

"Ah, well, surely you heard the bells when you lived there."

Kerry's needles slipped, and he focused hard to get the yarn back on track. He didn't like to think of his years living with Wilbet or his former alpha's parents, but, yes, he'd heard the bells. "Of course. The neighbors rang them for their children, and the priests walked the streets with their little bells."

"Yes, exactly."

"But tell me what *you* liked best."

"There was a plum pie that our head

cook baked, and it was absolutely divine. The meal was nothing compared to the Autumn Nights feasts, of course, but I liked it better because there were so many more sweets on offer to lure in winter-fox. Though I remember not understanding why we still needed to *lure* him back when he'd already come and left the gifts behind. I suppose I still don't understand that part." Janus smiled, his eyes going soft with memories, but then they cleared. "To tell you the truth, though, I like the mountain version better. The homecooked meals made to serve at a small table, just for family. The way the bells spill around the mountains and bounce off the lake. It feels homey and right. Like magic."

"But in the city, it's magic, too," Kerry offered. "Even if it's more evident that it's people doing the ringing, and the feast is shared more widely with guests and friends being invited."

"Yes, there's a certain sense of community in it. But nothing like here in the mountains, where you can practically feel the families delighting in their children's joy. In the city, there was an element of showing off for your guests—look at the wonderful toys we bought our children, look at the feast we can give."

"Amongst the wealthy, maybe, but in the Calitan district, things must surely be different."

Janus smiled. "Yes. I suppose."

"What was your favorite part of the holiday when you were little?"

"Like any child, my favorite part was the presents. Winter-fox had very extravagant taste in my family."

Kerry smiled. "I can imagine."

"I'm glad our Tristan will have more manageable expectations. He'll love the wagon your pater built for him and the new boots I got for him while I was in town. Though wolf-god knows I'll have to make another trip in just a few months at the rate he's growing."

Kerry nodded. "And Caleb sent those fluffy toy wildcats. We should have returned them. He sends us too much."

Janus waved his hand at that. "Caleb has more than enough, and he enjoys spreading the joy. He cares for us and loves Tristan. Let him spoil us some. It isn't going to hurt anyone."

"If we aren't careful, Tristan will think Caleb is winter-fox."

"Ah."

Kerry's cheeks felt hot. He wasn't going to look up from his knitting now. His prior jealousy of Caleb's former place in Janus's heart was completely resolved. He would *not* admit that some of that had transferred to jealousy with regards to Tristan's enthusiasm for the man.

It was just that whenever his "Uncle Caleb" visited, Tristan's excitement was unparalleled, and every word out of Caleb's mouth was considered as good as wolf-god's own truth, as far as Tristan was concerned. Caleb would never have been quizzed about whether the heart beating in his chest was truly his own.

Kerry wished his love for his son wasn't always touched with some kind of bitterness.

"Tristan will always love you best."

Kerry shrugged, embarrassed that Janus, as always, saw right through him.

"*I* love you best," Janus said.

"Like you have a choice," Kerry teased.

"I chose you," Janus insisted. "Before we knew what we were to each other, before we understood we were *Érosgápe*, I chose you."

Kerry put his knitting aside, shifting on the sofa until his head rested where his feet had been, pillowed on Janus's lap. He closed his eyes as Janus slipped his fingers through Kerry's long hair and trailed slow, tantalizing circles over his forehead and temples. Kerry practically purred.

"Say you chose *me*," Janus whispered.

"My heart's only ever belonged to you," Kerry said.

"Be careful. Tristan will think I stole it."

Kerry shrugged. "Maybe you did. As you said, he's smart."

Janus bent low and kissed Kerry, and time slipped away until they broke apart, naked, spent, and panting on the floor by the couch, the chiming clock reminding them of their duties. They washed off in the downstairs bathroom typically reserved for their boarding house's guests' use. There was no need to worry about guests barging in on them tonight, though; they'd closed up shop for a private, family holiday week.

Once clean, they returned to the living room, and set out the gifts.

Kerry carefully placed Caleb's fluffy toy wildcats in the shiny, new wagon. They looked happy waiting there for Tristan to discover them in the morning. He pushed aside his jealousy and took a moment to be grateful that his son had an "uncle" to spoil him in this way.

Winter-fox was going to be deeply generous to Tristan his first year celebrating.

CHAPTER TWO

THE NEXT MORNING the sun woke Janus by streaming through the windows and directly into his eyes. He groaned and sat up blearily, wondering about the time. Kerry was curled on his side facing Janus, his long, dark hair flung over the pillow, and his features slack with sleep.

It was the morning of the Feast of Winter's Heart, and it seemed impossible that Tristan hadn't already woken them so he could go down to see his gifts. Janus slipped from the bed, leaving Kerry still dreaming, and pulled on his robe. After pissing in the attached bathroom, he stepped out in the cold, morning hallway, listening hard. Perhaps his pater-in-law, Zeke, had gone down with Tristan and left Janus and Kerry to sleep in.

But there were no sounds from downstairs or the kitchen. Plus, Tristan's door stood open, but Zeke's was still shut, and there was something troubling about that.

Janus shuddered. A cold wind whipped up the staircase and down the hall, chilling him to the bone. With just a few quick steps, he was in Tristan's room. The bed was empty, covers tossed aside. No sweet face greeted him from the floor by the toy chest either.

Another rush of cold wind made Janus turn around to rush to the first floor. There, in the entry hall, he found the front door wide open. Outside, morning sun bounced off a pad of thick snow. It'd fallen overnight, and more was still coming down.

Had Tristan left the house? How long had he been outside? In this weather, he could…

Janus couldn't bear to think of it. He strode to the doorway, heart in his throat.

There! Tristan's footsteps broke the virgin snow. Thankfully, from the prints, it seemed he was wearing shoes.

Turning to the hall closet, Janus grabbed his own boots. As he put them on, along with his thickest coat, he noted that Tristan's wasn't hanging on the lower peg like usual. At least the boy wasn't out in the elements wearing just his pajamas.

Keenly aware that beneath his coat and robe *he* wore only lightweight pajamas himself, he dashed headlong into the yard, crunching heavily through the snow.

Rounding the corner of the house, he spotted his child almost immediately. Tristan stood not far from the edge of the wooded path which led down to the recently iced-over Hud's Basin.

"Look Father!" Tristan said, grinning. In his arms he held a black-spotted, baby wildcat. "Look what winter-fox brought for me!"

Janus's heart stopped. Memories of another morning on the very same path coming to mind.

He darted a rapid look around for the mother wildcat who was, undoubtedly, watching from the woods and was about attack Tristan at any moment to save her kitten.

"Tristan, put the cat down, and come to me. Slowly." He swallowed hard, keeping his eyes focused on the dark winter woods. He didn't see the mother cat yet, but she had to be there.

"He's skinny," Tristan said, hugging the cat to his chest. The animal didn't protest. "But he's mine."

"No, his mother will be back for him any moment, and she'll hurt you to protect him."

"He's been crying all night. I heard him," Tristan said stubbornly. "He's cold and hungry. I won't leave him, Father."

"Tristan," Janus put as much command into his voice as he could. His heart pounded so loudly he could barely hear himself speak. "Put the kitten down and come to me slowly."

Tristan narrowed his gaze, a bullish look coming over his face.

"Tristan," Kerry's voice came from behind Janus.

Glancing over his shoulder, Janus saw his beloved dressed in nothing but his thin pajamas and hastily pulled on boots. With his fragile lungs, he had no business being out in the cold like this. Janus needed to get Kerry and their obstinate son inside.

"Tristan," Kerry said again, his voice hard as steel. "Put the cat down. Come here. Now."

Tristan shook his head.

With swift steps, hindered only by the snow, Kerry stalked past Janus, dodging Janus's attempt to grab his arm, and swooped up his son. The kitten stayed stubbornly in the boy's arms as Tristan wailed into the hills, the sound bouncing off the trees.

"Winter-fox brought him for me! He's mine!"

Kerry clutched the struggling Tristan close, which was difficult since the boy was so big for his age, and rushed past Janus for the safety of the house. The kitten screeched and wailed, too. No doubt summoning its mother and her wrath at any moment.

Janus raced after his omega and son, barely making it inside before Kerry threw the door shut. He dumped his son and the kitten to the entryway floor, and sank down in relief, back pressed to the wall.

Janus stood panting with his heart in his throat, his own back to the closed door as if to keep a rampaging mother cat out. The kitten cried piteously, and so did Tristan.

"Damn wildcats," Kerry snapped.

"He's mine!" Tristan said again. "Winter-fox—"

"No!" Kerry shook all over. Even his

long hair trembled.

Remarkably, Tristan—wearing only his pajamas, his coat, and the new boots from winter-fox which had cost a nice number of coins—didn't seem cold at all. He held the kitten closer.

Zeke's tread thundered down the stairs, before he appeared in his robe with messy bedhead and a wild look in his eyes. "What in wolf-god's own hellish tarnation is going on down here?"

"Winter-fox brought me—" Tristan shouted, just as Kerry said, "My lunatic son—" and they all, including Janus, gestured at the baby wildcat.

"Oh!" Zeke gulped, staring. "I see."

The kitten was still crying, but it had stopped struggling and was now pressed up against Tristan, nearly as big as a fat sheepdog pup on his lap. Tristan buried his face in the cat's fur, and they all gasped, fully expecting the kitten to bite or scratch. But it did no such thing. Instead, after a quiet second, it began to purr.

The hallway filled with the sound.

"Well, wolf-god, what do we do now?" Zeke asked.

"HE COULD BE sick," Pater said. "And his mother abandoned him."

Kerry ran his fingers through his long, sleep-tangled hair. He studied Tristan where he snoozed on the rug by the fire, thumb in his mouth, and with the kitten curled up next to him.

After a few moments of debate in the hallway, they'd retreated to the warm kitchen and given the poor animal milk to lap up and a handful of cubed, raw meat. The kitten had eaten it all and then run to Tristan again, as if the boy were his mother.

For his part, Tristan ate his traditional holiday breakfast of warm oats and honey and a bit of bacon from the stores in the freezer. That had been a generous gift from Janus's side of the family in the fall, along with the news that they'd purchased the electrical station at the base of the mountain and removed the access limits to the people of the mountain. No more rationing of lights at night, and the new freezer was a welcome transition from the icebox.

Now the adults of the family sat in the living room, musing on what to do next.

"We can't just send him back out into the snow," Janus said, scraping a hand over his stubble. It glowed light gold in the firelight. "Tristan would never forgive us."

"He'd survive the disappointment," Kerry said softly. "The real question is whether the cat would. We can't know if his mother is out there looking for him, or if she's abandoned him, or if she is perhaps dead herself."

Pater clicked his tongue and then sighed. "We should put him out by the woods for a few hours. See if his mother comes for him."

"Tristan says he was out there all night," Janus said. "Crying for his mother."

Kerry sighed. "Fan told me last week that Pax was hunting wildcats for his new omega mate. You know, the one he found over on Yonder Mountain."

"Why?" Janus asked.

"His omega likes the taste of cat over deer, apparently. Grew up on it over on his ridge. Says the meat's tastier." Kerry shrugged. "And Pax doesn't mind trapping them because the cats got to his chickens this past summer, so he's got a grudge about the lost eggs. Fan also said Pax had already bagged five big ones but wanted a few more."

"Why does he need so many? I know many men prefer to hunt over bringing the slaughterhouse meat up from town, but surely between the deer he's got and these five cats, he has enough now?"

"Pax's omega is pregnant, and Fan thinks it's twins. Going to be a rough delivery for him, and his alpha wants him fat and hardy going into it. If he can tempt him to eat more…"

Janus nodded, and Kerry knew he'd be exactly the same way when, or if, Kerry ever got pregnant again. Back when he'd been large with Tristan, eating hadn't been a problem, but he knew many omegas felt sick far into the pregnancy, endangering their lives and the baby's life, too. Twins…wolf-god, Kerry couldn't even imagine. Carrying and giving birth to Tristan alone had been enough to scare him away from having another child any time soon. Thankfully Janus wasn't averse to using alpha condoms and took care during heats not to get Kerry pregnant.

Though maybe one day Kerry would ask for another son. When Tristan was older. When the memories had faded a little more.

Silence fell over the room. They all studied the kitten and the chubby-cheeked boy all cuddled up with it.

"He can't keep it," Kerry said after many long minutes had passed. "It's not safe for Tristian or right for the animal."

"But we can't leave it out in the cold to die either," Janus muttered. "It's not old enough to fend for itself."

"The longer we let it stay in the house, the more attached the little one'll get," Pater warned. "Should you even be letting him sleep with it now? Its teeth and claws are plenty sharp."

No one moved, though. The cat exuded sweetness and peace, his head resting on Tristan's outstretched arm. And Tristan looked like an angel with his light hair shining in the firelight and his rosy cheeks moving as he sucked on his thumb. Kerry both hoped he outgrew the habit soon and dreaded the loss of yet another piece of Tristan's babyhood. Time moved so quickly.

"What are we going to call it?" Janus asked.

And just like that, Kerry knew their fate

was sealed.

Tristan would keep the cat, and they would find a way to make it work. Janus, his determined alpha, had chosen their course.

"I suppose we should let Tristan choose," Kerry said, turning to his yarn and needles. A strange peace settled over him despite knowing the entire morning had been nothing but madness and that they had much to figure out regarding the care of a wildcat kitten. "After all, winter-fox brought it for him."

The fire crackled, the kitten stirred, and Janus nodded in ponderous silence. Pater rose from his chair, stretched his back, and then headed without a word into the kitchen to begin preparations for the Feast of Winter's Heart. Already accepting the change. Already willing to adapt. That was what Kerry's pater did, after all.

And that was what Kerry aimed to do, too. It was what he'd *learned* to do.

CHAPTER THREE
TRISTAN, AGE 6

One Year Later

"BUT PATER, IT'S so cold tonight," Tristan said, stuffing his hands into his coat pockets. He'd stopped sucking his thumb ages ago, but he felt the urge to shove it in his mouth now as he gazed at the "den" his father and pater had built for Chewy, his own special cat.

Pater put his arm around Tristan's shoulder and drew him close to his body, which was round now with the baby that was on the way. A little brother for him to love. Tristan couldn't wait to hold him and snuggle him and kiss his fat cheeks. But he was also a little mad at the baby, too. It was his fault, after all, that Chewy had to live outside now. "He'll be fine, sweet boy. He's made to live outside in a den, and your father insulated it well with moss and mud, and he put in the soft, old blankets that Chewy slept on in the pantry."

The blankets *were* soft. Tristan knew because two or three nights a week, he slept in them with Chewy on the floor. Something he'd have to stop doing now that they were moving Chewy outside.

Yes, Chewy had grown quite big, but he was still a cub by wildcat standards. He'd still be living with his mother if she hadn't left him in the snow, probably caught by that big alpha Pax's hunting traps. Chewy would still be learning the ways of the wildcat life from her. He was just a little boy cat, like Tristan was a little boy human, and he needed his family.

"Sweetheart, let's go inside." Pater shuddered. The night was crystal clear and without snow. Stars shone above. The mountains were gray smudges against the blackness of the sky. "The bells will start soon. You'll want to join in."

Tristan followed his pater inside, casting longing glances back to the wooden "den" covered in moss and mud and leaves and wondering what would happen if Chewy didn't stay inside, if he wandered out into the night. The other wildcats might not like him. They might not make friends.

"Will winter-fox protect him?"

"He's meant to be outside," Pater said again, his voice firmer. "We can't keep him locked inside the house forever or tied to a leash in the yard. He'll grow miserable and waste away. This is best for him. He'll start to be more like a regular wildcat. And he's still here, near us, and we'll continue to help feed him. He'll be all right, Tristan. Let's go."

Reluctantly, Tristan left, wishing that Chewy would leave his cozy, new den and the soft blankets behind to follow Tristan inside. They were a team, the two of them. They were friends, and it hurt Tristan's heart that his wildcat seemed content in his new house.

"He wouldn't eat the baby," Tristan said when they finally sat down in the living room in front of the fire, warming up in advance of going out to the porch to ring the bells. The tree they'd brought inside and covered in colored paper and shiny bulbs that Uncle Caleb had sent glittered in the firelight. "I just know he wouldn't. Chewy would love the baby. Like he loves me."

Pater shifted uncomfortably, his hand on his stomach, and he grimaced before giving Father the look which meant he wanted him to handle Tristan's question.

Father sat with Pater's feet in his lap, rubbing them the way he often did. "Chewy is a good wildcat, but he's still a powerful animal. He isn't a typical pet."

Tristan shrugged. Of course Chewy

wasn't a typical pet. He was quite obviously special in every way. "Winter-fox brought him to us."

"Yes, and winter-fox would want him to live the best kind of life that a wildcat can live, and that means roaming free."

Tristan pouted. He knew deep down that Father was right, but it didn't make it any easier to give up the comfort of knowing his pet was safe inside the house at night.

"Speaking of winter-fox," Grandpater said, standing up from his comfortable chair and groaning softly. "It's comin' on time for the bells."

Tristan's heart leapt. Darting from the room and down the hall, he flung open the front door and stood on the porch. The cold air took his breath for a moment, but soon he had his hands on the bells Grandpater and Pater had hung up on nails by the door to be rung as the moon rose each night.

His parents were just behind him. They'd taken the time to pull on coats, and as the sound of the other families' ringing rose from out of the hills around him, Tristan passed the wooden-handled bells to his family, joy bubbling inside as he shook his again and again, too.

Once Pater had slipped a coat onto Tristan, Father lifted him up onto his shoulders. From the height of Father's shoulders, Tristan could see the moon above the decorated trees at the edge of the forest and the snow that had begun falling lightly all around. Pater stood close, his long hair moving in the breeze, and Grandpater huddled in as well. Together, as a family, they rang their bells, adding to the music in the air all around. Winter-fox was coming, and he was bringing something good. Tristan just knew it.

When it was time to be tucked into bed, Tristan snuggled into the soft warmth of his clean, fresh blankets. His father stroked his hair and told him that he loved him. Then his pater kissed his cheek and sang the lullaby that he loved best before turning out the light and leaving him alone. Tristan tried to sleep, but he couldn't shake the fizz and pop of excitement in his veins. He stood and went to the window, gazing out toward the hill where Chewy's den was, and waited. He didn't see any movement. Surely his cat was all right.

He crawled back into bed and finally, after tossing and turning, fell into a light sleep.

But when Tristan woke in the night, he was certain he'd heard a wildcat scream. He ran to the window and peered out toward Chewy's den, but there was nothing but the blue of starlight on new snow. Tristan left his room and headed down the hall on his tiptoes. He was surprised to see the light on under his parents' door. It was well into the night. There were strange, grunting sounds coming from inside. Whines and moans, too. He paused, considered knocking, and then remembered what his friend Remy at the

Hud's Basin school had told him: sometimes parents did the heat thing even when there was no heat.

That didn't bear thinking about.

Tristan crept down the stairs to the hall closet, grabbed his coat and boots, a hat and gloves, and then snuck into the living room to steal his pater's favorite blanket from the sofa. Bundled up, he left the house by the back entrance and stole down toward the den. He found it empty.

Crawling inside, he waited, his little heart pounding. The scream came in the night again, and he chewed on his bottom lip. Where was Chewy? Was he hurt? He sat as still as he could and waited. It was warm in the den like Pater and Father had promised. Quite warm.

He grew drowsy, and when he woke, Chewy was curled all around, and his father was shouting his name into the morning light.

"HE'S SO LITTLE," Tristan whispered, kissing his brother's head.

He'd been scolded roundly by his father for sneaking out into the night, which was a traumatizing thing in and of itself because Father never scolded him. That was Pater's job. But Pater was too tired after a long night of giving birth to his brother, and he was propped up in bed looking pale.

Tristan climbed up beside him, and Pater made room. They stared down at the sleeping baby together, with Father sitting on Pater's other side. The baby was awfully red and wrinkled, but his cheeks were very fat already, and his fingers were teeny versions of Tristan's own.

"He's beautiful," Father said.

Tristan shrugged. "If you like red and wrinkled, then I guess…"

Father reached over and slipped his

fingers through Tristan's hair. "You were red and wrinkled, too."

Tristan bent to kiss his brother's head again. "I'll love him even if he stays ugly."

Pater kissed Tristan's cheek and snuggled him in closer. They all breathed together quietly, watching the baby sleep.

"Look what winter-fox brought me," Tristan said to Grandpater when the moment was broken by his arrival. Grandpater was freshly showered and wearing clean clothes, but his eyes were hazy like he'd been up all night. "Don't worry, Grandpater. He's ugly now, but he'll be cute when he grows some. Father says so. Do you think it's true?"

"Yes, I do. What are we going to call him?" Grandpater smoothed a finger down the baby's soft, blotchy cheek.

Pater chuckled, and his voice sounded rougher than usual when he said, "We haven't decided, but one thing's for sure—we aren't letting Tristan decide."

Father scoffed. "You don't want a son

called Chewy the Second?"

"No, definitely not."

"I wouldn't name him Chewy," Tristan said, offended. He kissed his brother's cheek again. It was addictively soft. "I'd name him Zekial. After Grandpater."

Pater and Father looked at each other. The baby started to fuss. Pater opened his shirt, and Tristan watched in awe as the baby latched on and started to chestfeed hungrily. Nothing more was said for a long time.

But, as it turned out, Tristan named his baby brother after all.

CHAPTER FOUR

TRISTAN, AGE 10

Four Years Later

"ZEKIE, BE CAREFUL!" Tristan lunged toward where his four-year-old brother was teetering on a big rock outcropping by the edge of the lake.

But Chewy was there before Tristan could reach Zekial, leaping from the trees above and using his big cat body to butt the boy away from the not-yet-frozen water. Zekial started to cry, but Chewy continued to push him back away from the lake.

When Tristan reached them, he gave Chewy a pat and a nuzzle, before hefting

Zekial up into his arms. Tristan was big for his age—always had been—and Zekial was small. Since Tristan had started to present as an alpha early, he'd grown even stronger, with his muscles coming in before most other boys on the mountain. But Zekial was squirmy, and fussy, and, wolf-god, so annoying. It was hard to hold him.

"You can't go swimming without Pater or Father! And besides, it's winter and the water's cold. I've told you before."

Zekial let out a shriek, and Tristan rolled his eyes. That would bring Pater running for sure.

He'd only managed to half-carry and half-herd Zekial a few yards up the path when Pater came waddling down, dark hair flying behind him, and his jaw set. Tristan wanted to burrow against him and get hugs the way he used to, press his face against Pater's neck and breathe in his scent. But Tristan was too old for that now. He was too tall for even Father to carry. Pater hugged him now and again still, yes, but his comforting arms were usually full of Zekie these days, and, soon enough, they'd be full of the new baby that was growing inside.

Tristan could smell the change this time. His alpha senses were coming in, and he could make out how the baby changed Pater's overall odor to something more like Father, and more like Zekial, but altogether different, too. He felt a little jealous of that—knowing they were all family in every way. But then he'd see his Father's proud eyes on him, or Pater would come into his room late at night to smooth the hair off his forehead and whisper that he loved him, and Tristan would forget all about his fear that he wasn't a real Heelies, that maybe he was a Monhundy deep down inside. Whatever that meant.

All he really knew was that it meant something bad.

But those weren't good thoughts for the day before the Feast of Winter's Heart.

"What's going on?" Pater asked Tristan as Zekial broke into a wobbly run and buried his face against Pater's leg. He hauled the boy up into his arms and kissed his wet cheeks. "Why's he crying?"

"I wouldn't let him go swimming."

Pater's lips quirked. "He loves the water. Like me."

"I told him it was too cold and that he couldn't go in without you or Father, so he screamed."

"Toohey!" Zekial yelled, still sobbing, pointing behind Tristan at where Chewy prowled in the trees alongside the path. "Toohey pushed me!"

Pater raised a brow.

Tristan wet his lips. He had to tread lightly now. Pater was less lenient than Father about Chewy's role in his life. Along with being the one to scold most often, Pater was the one to worry the most. About Tristan's safety. About Zekial's safety. About whether wildcats belonged in a homemade den on the edge of their property, much less in Tristan's life as a pet of sorts.

"He kept him from falling in, Pater. That's all. Chewy saw that Zekie was heading into the water and cut him off. He saved him."

Pater nuzzled Zekial's hair and then nodded. "Chewy takes care of you both," he agreed. But he sounded tense about it. Tristan glanced toward the forest and saw that Chewy was slinking away into the brown and gray shadows.

No snow for the feast this year. None coming either. The air was warmer than usual, and the scent of mud clung to each breath.

With his Pater close by and doting, Zekial calmed enough that Pater put him down. Soothed and ready to play again, Zekial promptly started digging a hole with a stick off to the side of the path.

Pater motioned toward a rock that was big enough for them both to sit on, and

Tristan climbed up beside him. A sense of wonder filled him as his pater took hold of his hand and pressed it to his swelling belly. "Feel."

Tristan smiled. The baby was moving inside. The press of a foot or an elbow slid across Tristan's palm. "Does it hurt?" he asked.

"No. Well, sometimes, when he wedges himself against my ribs. But, otherwise, no."

Tristan felt the baby moving for a few quiet minutes as Zekial sang and dug and then started to fill his new hole with pebbles. "Do you think it'll be an omega this time?"

Pater shrugged. "I don't know. I hope not."

Tristan frowned. "Why?"

"It's hard to be an omega. I'm grateful that you and Zekial will be able to make choices about your life without having to worry about heats."

"But I'll have to worry about my omega's heats."

Pater smiled softly. "If you find your *Érosgápe*, yes, I suppose so. But if you don't…well, you don't have to contract with *any* omega. Your future is yours to choose. And your brother's, too."

"Do you think Zekie is a beta, or an alpha like me?"

Pater shrugged again. "I don't know. Time will tell."

Tristan didn't think Zekial was an alpha. Or maybe he just thought so because his brother was so much younger. Pater was right. Only time would tell.

"Will you be sad, though, if this one is an omega?"

Pater stilled for a moment, and then he put his arm around Tristan. "No. I'll teach him to value himself and understand that with the right alpha, life can be beautiful."

"With his *Érosgápe*, you mean."

"Maybe, but it doesn't have to be. An alpha should cherish his omega, even if they aren't *Érosgápe*. An alpha should love and protect him."

Tristan nodded solemnly. "I will do that for my omega one day. I promise."

Pater kissed his hair and smiled. Pride pierced Tristan to the heart. He'd made Pater happy. He loved doing that. "I know you will, sweet boy. I count on it." Pater touched his stomach. "And this baby will be loved so deeply. He'll have a father and pater and two big brothers who'll make sure that if he's an omega, whatever contract he signs, it's with someone who will cherish him beyond all else."

"I promise to protect him always," Tristan said, realizing that this was what Pater wanted him to say.

"Good." He glanced toward where Zekial was now adding acorns to the pile of pebbles in the hole. "Now, Tristan. We need to talk about Chewy…"

"No, Pater." Tristan slid off the rock and stood up, crossing his arms over his chest. "He's mine. Winter-fox entrusted him to me, just like you're entrusting me with my brothers. I won't make him go away."

Pater's lips quirked. "I'm not sure you could even if you tried."

"Then what do you want me to do?"

Pater patted the spot next to him. "Did I ever tell you about my bird?"

Tristan slowly sat again, and then he leaned against his pater, scenting his hair and the skin of his neck. He loved him so much that it made his heart hurt. "Yes, but you can tell me again."

"Do you remember that day, Tristan? The day the wildcat was going to pounce on you?"

"I was little, but I remember the funeral for Kiwi."

"Yes, Kiwi. My beautiful bird. I'd set him free, but he never left me. Not really. Then he saved you from that wildcat. I think Chewy is like Kiwi. He wants to take care of you. He thinks of you as *his*."

"And Zekie, too."

"Maybe. I know he'd never hurt you or Zekial on purpose, but he's a big cat and you must be careful. Always remember he's wild and belongs in the forest. He's not going to think like you. He can't."

"I know."

"And it's possible he'll want to mate one day, and if and when he does, he might change."

"How?"

"He might not trust you with his kittens. Or his mate might not. Wildcat mothers are…" Pater smiled and touched Tristan's cheek. "Well, they're like paters. They'll do anything to protect their little ones from harm. Risk anything for them, too."

"I understand, Pater. I promise I'll be careful with Chewy, and make sure Zekie's careful with him, too."

"So many promises from you today," Pater said with a trace of humor. "Come now. Let's all go back inside, and you can help your grandpater with cooking. You know he's getting too old to do it all on his own, and I'm worthless in the kitchen."

Zekial kicked up a fuss about leaving his acorn and pebble-filled hole, but when the words plum tart were mentioned, he stopped his sobbing and started running up the path on his fat little legs.

Pater followed, and Tristan took the rear, keeping an eye on his pater to make sure he was safe getting up the path with his cumbersome stomach. The baby was big this time, and Father was worried about the birth. Even Tristan could see that. But Pater was relaxed about it and told them all that he had a good feeling that it would be an easy one.

Tristan hoped his pater was right.

THE BELLS WERE special the last night leading up to the Feast of Winter's Heart. It was the first time Zekie understood what they were all about, and his excitement for winter-fox was unparalleled. Getting Zekie put to bed was nigh on impossible, and Tristan sat patiently awake in his own room until the household had settled. Then he did as he had every Eve of the Feast of Winter's Heart since he was six years old.

He crept out of the house with his blanket, coat, hat, and gloves and went down to Chewy's den. He'd passed the living room on his way, smiling to see the things his parents had put out for his brother, as well as the shiny, wrapped packages that had to be new clothes for him.

Yes, new clothes sent from Uncle Caleb…for the new school in the town at the bottom of the mountain, the one they were sending him to in the spring. New clothes for the next stage of his life.

Tristan ducked his head into the den and found it empty. That wasn't uncommon these days. Wildcats were mostly nocturnal after all, and Chewy was probably out looking for his dinner.

Tristan got comfortable inside the cozy space, though it was harder than it had been in years past when he was a smaller boy. Once Chewy joined him, there would be very little room for them both, but they'd be snug and warm. Tristan couldn't wait to bury his face in Chewy's warm fur, breathe in his animal scent, and sleep next to his friend.

The sounds of the night drifted into the den—an owl hooting, the trees creaking. His eyes grew heavy. He let himself drift off, knowing that soon, very soon, Chewy would come to him.

But morning dawned, and Tristan woke alone.

There was no voice calling for him. No shouts of worry. He was damp and a little chilled on the den floor, and Chewy was nowhere to be found. Tristan crawled out of the den and stretched. He took a sullen step forward and then stopped. There on the ground at his feet was a dead rabbit with

Chewy's paw prints all around.

Tristan grimaced as he picked up the gift and held it aloft. It was in good condition. He could skin it and give it to his grandpater for stew. He gazed around, looking for his wildcat but saw no trace of him. He headed toward the back of the house nursing his disappointment that Chewy hadn't honored their Feast of Winter's Heart ritual.

As if Chewy could have known…

Tristan left the rabbit on the back porch and then went inside to clean up for the day ahead. He couldn't wait to see his little brother's face when he saw the fun things their Uncle Caleb had sent for him and the items their parents had gotten him, too. He was more excited about Zekie's gifts than he was for his own.

The morning slipped by. In the brilliance of Zekie's joy, the rabbit and Chewy were forgotten, only remembered when Tristan followed Zekial outside to watch the surprise snowfall coming down. The rabbit was where he'd left it. And Chewy's den was still empty.

That night Tristan waited by the den for a long time, snow dusting his shoulders as he listened hard for the snap of branches in the wood, wondering where Chewy had gone— wondering if he'd be back by morning.

Tristan didn't see Chewy that night.

Or that entire next year.

Or the next.

Or the next.

Or the next.

CHAPTER FIVE

TRISTAN AGE 18

Eight Years Later

"THIS IS THE best present ever!" Zekial shouted, lifting up a small medical kit.

Max pushed toy soldiers into formation beneath the table next to the sofa, and tiny Hudson rolled from his front to his back again on the baby blanket next to the decorated pine tree. It was his new trick, and the baby laughed every time he did it.

"Nah," Tristan said, pushing his hair off his forehead and winking at his brother. "Winter-fox brought me the best present ever years ago. Yours is *maybe* second best."

Zekie rolled his eyes, *his* new favorite trick. "I mean, it's true. I was a great present."

"Not you. My wildcat."

Zekie scoffed. "After all these years, I can't believe you still claim winter-fox brought you a baby wildcat."

"He did," Tristan asserted.

"Did not," Max piped up, mainly because he always took Zekial's side in any argument with Tristan.

The baby, too young to gang up yet, gurgled and laughed again.

"Did too," Tristan muttered, flushing with frustration that he'd fallen into their childish ways.

He was grown now. Too old for winter-fox to bring him things anymore. Old enough to be leaving the mountain in a few months to go live with Uncle Caleb and his alphas in the city. He was going to attend university in the fall to prepare for the rest of his life. And he was almost old enough to meet his *Érosgápe*, too. He was a grown alpha. He shouldn't be falling for his younger brothers' attempts to pick a fight.

"His name was Chewy, and he was a good wildcat."

"Chewy," Max repeated under his breath before sending his toy soldiers into some violent battle that resulted in all of them being slaughtered by the looks of it.

Zekial continued going through his medical case carefully, taking out all kinds of instruments. He'd been going up mountain with their father for several months now, training in rudimentary medicine and learning herbs with Dr. Crescent's omega, Fan. He was a beta, or so it seemed, with no evidence of presenting as an alpha as he passed through puberty, so there was no need for him to attend university if he didn't want to. He could learn a trade now and start his life...

Tristan just hoped he wouldn't be lonely.

Betas weren't long for the mountain, usually. Most of them left for more opportunities in the city, searching for beta partners with whom they could make a life. The mountains encouraged families and homesteads, and a family was one thing a beta could never make, only find.

"Chewy kept you from drowning in the lake," Tristan said, softly to Zekial. "The last day I ever saw him. You don't even remember."

Zekial put aside the kit and stretched. "Why would I have drowned if you were there to save me?"

Tristan smirked. He wondered how Zekial would do without him on the mountain next year. He too often depended on Tristan to look out for him, protect him against the bullies at the town school. Always had.

"Chewy was a good cat," Pater said from where he was knitting on the sofa, his feet in Father's lap. "And he was a real cat, too,

Zekial. Not just a figment of Tristan's imagination."

"I figured as much," Zekial said, conceding that he'd just been teasing to get a rise out of his older brother. "All animals love him, like he's some fairytale prince. He raised that baby squirrel, remember? And he took care of that fox kit until he healed." He smiled fondly at Tristan. "I just like to rile him up. That's what little brothers are for, right? You'll miss me in the city, won't you?"

Tristan nodded, a lump forming in his throat. He would.

And he hated that he'd miss Hudson growing up altogether.

Tristan had been in the room when Hudson was born, caught him in his own hands. He felt a special affinity for the baby after helping him slip out into the world from their Pater's body. Father had been sick again with the flu, and Dr. Crescent had been too slow to arrive, so Tristan had been the one to help his Pater labor, with Zekie doing a great job at backup. Tristan understood why his Father wanted to train Zekial in medicine. He'd been calm and steady throughout the whole event.

So had Tristan, though he'd been running on adrenaline and terror the whole time. Tristan's awe of his pater had only grown in the aftermath—to endure so much pain and live! To push life from his body like that! Unreal!

And now Hudson was fat and rolling around on the carpet, a little ball of joy. Pater was resilient and recovered, and, thankfully, Father was healthy and strong again, too. Though Dr. Crescent said he needed to avoid more bouts of flu at all costs. He'd suffered too many of them in his life. Tristan's eyes filled at the thought of his father getting sick again. It'd been such a close call, and Pater had been beside himself in fear. *Érosgápe* suffered most when their beloveds grew sick or, worse, died.

"Oh, don't cry," Zekie said, scooting

across the carpet to hook his arm around Tristan's neck and tug him in for a hug. "I know you'll miss me, but wolf-god…don't cry about it. Such a soft heart. Don't let them chew you up in the city."

Pater's knitting needles stopped clacking, and a haunted expression flitted over his face. Then he cleared his throat and said, "Caleb will look after you. He's assured me you'll be fine in the city."

Tristan smiled, even though he did still feel like crying. "I'll be all right, Pater. I promise."

Pater nodded, but he put aside his knitting and scooped Hudson up from the carpet, immediately plugging up his disturbed fussing by chestfeeding him. Pater did that sometimes when he wanted to calm himself or act like everything was normal.

When he wanted to act like Tristan wasn't on his way out the door.

Father said there were hormones released during chestfeeding that caused automatic relaxation in omegas, and as Tristan watched his Pater feed Hudson, he saw his tense shoulders ease.

In the light of the fire, Father studied Tristan carefully. "Tell me, what will you do in the city if the Monhundys come looking for you?"

The lump of tender sadness in Tristan's throat turned to thick dread. "Summon Uncle Caleb."

"Or my cousins, Xan or his older brother Ray. Whatever you do, don't go anywhere with anyone from that family. Call the police if you need to, so you can be safe."

"I know," Tristan whispered.

"You're *my* son," Father said. "Don't forget that. Ever."

"Never," Tristan said.

Zekial hugged Tristan around the neck again. "C'mon, it's Feast of Winter's Heart today. Let's not turn this into another sobfest about how our precious Tristan is leaving us."

Tristan elbowed him, but Zekial kissed Tristan's cheek before abandoning him to help Max with his soldiers. The room fell quiet except for the sound of the fire crackling and Max making the rat-a-tat noises of his toy soldiers' guns.

No one mentioned it, but Tristan could have sworn they were all thinking of Grandpater in that moment, as if his ghost had crept into the room to look in on his little family again. Tristan missed Grandpater, but at least his final illness had been quick, and he hadn't suffered. That's what mattered most, Father said. That and the love they'd shared as a family over the years.

"Who's going to cook the feasts when I'm gone?" Tristan asked, unable to hold back the question now that it'd come to his mind. He and Grandpater had always made the meals for Autumn Nights, and for the Feast of Winter's Heart, and Tristan was in charge of preparing the meal that day.

"I'm gonna learn," Max said from beneath the table, his small voice bright. "Fan's gonna teach me."

"Oh, he is?" Tristan said with a laugh. "Is he going to teach you to add in special herbs, too?"

"Don't make fun of Fan," Zekial said.

Tristan held up his hands. "I'd never."

"Hey now," Father said. "Everyone play nicely."

It was an old phrase, one that Tristan wouldn't be hearing much anymore. Not when he left. "Well, come on then, let's get started on your learning now. I'll teach you how to make the plum tarts."

Max shoved the soldiers aside willingly and took Tristan's hand. He gazed up at Tristan with wide, worshipful eyes as they walked to the kitchen to begin. Tristan's heart ached.

He was going to miss his family so much.

CHAPTER SIX
TRISTAN, AGE 19

One Year Later

NOTHING WAS THE same in the city.

Tristan had learned *that* when he first arrived at his Uncle Caleb's house. Well, actually, the large mansion in one of the nicest areas of town belonged to Janus's cousin, Xan. But the familial relationships were complicated by contracts, friendships, and old grudges, not to mention by Tristan not being Janus's child by blood. And so it was that his father's cousin, Xan, felt more like a stranger than the omega Xan had contracted with, and whom Tristan called uncle.

The night hung with a soft fog, eerie and deep, obscuring even the houses just across the street. Tristan waited on the massive front portico, ready for the celebration to start. None of Caleb and Xan's five children were still young enough to celebrate the Feast of Winter's Heart, but there would be bells to hear every night this week. Tristan waited with a thick coat and a scarf wrapped around his throat to keep the wet chill away.

The front door opened behind him, and Tristan's heart lifted.

It must be Bek—his age mate in the house and his closest friend. Even if Bek was a beta and already learning a trade in his father's business, and Tristan was in university learning his place as the dominant gender, they were still close. Few people in the city had made Tristan feel as welcome as Bek. Most, including his classmates, made him feel stupid and ignorant, like mountain trash.

"Here to listen to the bells?" Tristan asked, smiling as he turned.

Instead of Bek, though, he found beautiful, black-haired Riki, wrapped in a red coat and shining brighter than a fire in the darkness. Tristan's breath caught in his throat, captivated by the stunning blue eyes which gleamed in Riki's pale face and by the dark curls trained carefully around his high cheekbones.

Riki.

Xan and Caleb's eldest, omega son. Tall and lithe, quiet and cultured, Riki made Tristan's heart ache in ways he didn't understand. And in the dark of the night, Tristan had to admit, his treacherous cock wanted Riki, too. It rushed hot with blood and rose stiffly beneath his heavy, wool coat.

Tristan hated how his body betrayed him. It wasn't as though they were *Érosgápe*—not as far as Tristan could tell. He didn't scent anything perfect in Riki, no delicious wisp of heaven as he'd heard the

Érosgápe's scent described by their destined mates. And Riki didn't react to Tristan at all. He behaved as if Tristan were just any younger alpha relative—boring, juvenile, and possibly stupid. All Tristan's books and classes had let him know that his *Érosgápe* would leak slick for him, feel drawn to him, and return his need once they'd found each other. Riki seemed to barely know Tristan was alive.

No, during Tristan's months in the Heelies house, he'd found that Riki's attention was focused on one thing and one thing only: Viro Sabel.

Viro was the alpha son of Riki's parents' best friends, and was, according to Bek, Riki's intended—assuming neither of them found their *Érosgápe* before the year's end. Their parents were delighted. Riki was in love. And Viro—well, Tristan had never met Viro, but he'd seen pictures, and the alpha was beyond impressive. Handsome, charismatic even in photos, and morally upright according to the general consensus of the family.

Viro had graduated from Mont Nessadare a few years back. But rather than spending the next few years seeking his *Érosgápe* at Philia soirees, he'd taken a more active approach, traveling the world and meeting omegas from all corners. Based on the dinner conversation Tristan had overheard about it all, Riki seemed to find this pursuit amusing and exciting but not exactly threatening to his plans. Instead, he reveled in Viro's movements, claiming Viro had no intention of ever settling down in the city or working a boring job at his father's company. No, Viro would *travel* and *pray* and *help the indigent* and take Riki with him into the great wide yonder, and Tristan didn't like how he felt about all that.

At all.

Realizing he'd been staring, Tristan cleared his throat and rubbed a hand over his face. "Uh, hi…are you…uh—"

"Do you mind if I join you?" Riki asked, putting Tristan out of his misery. His voice was soft, almost a whisper, and he didn't look at Tristan as he asked, staring into the fog with a moody expression.

"Of course. The bells should start soon."

"Yes, very soon."

They stood in awkward silence, but Tristan could feel each of Riki's breaths, the slight hitch in them as if he might be about to cry. "What's wrong?" he asked, worried that the bells would start to ring and cover whatever Riki's answer might be.

"Nothing," Riki said. His long fingers twitched through the black curls on his pale forehead. "Just…people." He huffed a hurt-sounding laugh. "They can be so horrible. It's a wonder wolf-god saw fit to save us at all."

Tristan nodded but said nothing more. He didn't know what to say. It was true people in the city were often assholes. He'd been shocked at times by the self-absorbed bitterness so many people expressed through their words and actions. Mountain folks would never treat each other in such ways. But he'd been taught long ago, by his Grandpater, not to say anything negative to city people about their habits or their ways, even when invited to do so.

So, he kept his mouth shut now, too.

"They're saying Sam isn't Father's son again," Riki said under his breath. "The omegas at his school, I mean."

"Oh?" Tristan licked his lips. It was obvious Sam wasn't the son of Xan's loins. He thought everyone knew that? But he wasn't going to say it aloud if it would upset Riki.

"Because of his skin."

Tristan swallowed and nodded. "Yes. His skin is quite dark."

Riki blew out a harsh breath. "Well, of course, he's Urho's. I'm not stupid, but it upsets Sam to hear people gossip about it."

"Xan loves him and claims him as his own," Tristan said softly. His father had done the same for him, and it'd meant the world as he grew up, but he also knew the sharpness of doubt—was he really Janus's son? Or was he a Monhundy?

"Yes…" Riki growled under his breath. "It makes me want to punch people. Do you ever want to just *punch* people, Tristan?"

The fog around them shifted and swirled. Tristan looked into Riki's eyes, dazzled by the sharp blueness, and cleared his throat. "Not usually. No."

But if it would make Riki happy, if it would make him smile, Tristan would punch a dozen people. Just point him at them. And if those people had upset Riki and Sam? Then they probably deserved it.

Riki smiled, and just the sight of his sharp canine teeth did absolutely cruel things to Tristan's soul. "No? You're sweet. Most alphas our age aren't as sweet as you."

Tristan's heart hammered, his hands went cold and clammy in his gloves, and he could barely breathe. He wanted to tell Riki how sweet he was, too, that he was beautiful, and handsome, and so smart. Too smart for a mountain alpha like Tristan…

And yet he wanted him…*so much*. But he kept his mouth shut because he wasn't an idiot.

"Here," Riki said, taking Tristan's arm. "Let's sit."

The front step of the portico was cold on his ass, but it helped cool him, too. His heart throbbed as he sat with Riki and waited. When the bells started ringing in wolf-god's churches and then began to echo in the fog around them, tinkling from porches, clanging from windows, and jangling in the hands of priests in the streets, Tristan felt as if he were hallucinating.

Riki sat pressed against him, arm looped through his, and his dark head resting on Tristan's shoulder. The bells rang and sang, and his heart hammered, his blood pounded, and he wanted to shout in joy. He wanted to clutch Riki closer and scream with need, but he stayed still.

When the bells fell silent, the fog began to slowly lift. Yet Riki continued to sit beside Tristan.

Just as Tristan was about to explode from indecision about what to do next, Riki asked, "What's the Feast of Winter's Heart like in the mountains?"

"Calmer," Tristan said. "Not nearly so loud. But maybe more magical." His voice trembled. He hoped Riki didn't notice.

"What was the best present winter-fox ever brought you?" Riki asked.

"I should say my brother Zekial, but he's actually a big pain in my ass."

Riki laughed. It was more beautiful than all the bells of the night.

Tristan went on, "My best gift was a wildcat kitten. I named him Chewy, and I had him for five years."

"Really? That's...the most mountain-folk thing I've ever hear you say."

Tristan shrugged, his soaring joy damp-ening slightly.

But then Riki turned to him, his face quite close and utterly beautiful. "So, what happened to him?"

"Chewy left me on the Eve of the Feast of Winter's Heart when I was ten. I don't know why he left, where he went, or if he lived, or if he died. I don't know what became of him."

"How sad. An unsolved mystery."

"I suppose we all have some of those in our lives," Tristan said, thinking again of his blood father. Where was he? Did he know Tristan lived? Did he care? "Where Chewy came from and where he went, I'll never know."

Riki nodded, gazing up at Tristan with a new expression. "Where will *you* go, Tristan? When you've done what you've come here to do. Back to the mountains?"

Tristan licked his lips and had to restrain himself from replying, *"I don't know, but I'd go anywhere with you."* Instead, he murmured, "I suppose I'll let my omega help me decide."

Riki's brows twitched. "You'd do that? Give him a say?"

"Of course."

"Viro says we'll go wherever his heart leads us."

Tristan dared to touch Riki's cheek, pretending to brush off a bit of dirt. He felt like he might swoon. "But what about where *your* heart leads?"

Riki's gaze flitted down to Tristan's lips. The moment grew thick as the fog. Tristan felt dizzy with hope. And then Riki pulled back, stood up, and brushed off the seat of his long coat. "It's over now. The bells, I mean. I'll see you at the breakfast table tomorrow. Good night, Tristan."

And just like that, Riki was gone again.

Tristan sat on the front step, aching to his bones, and wishing he'd said something different. Wishing he'd found a way to make Riki want to stay.

Wishing winter-fox would bring him a cure for his pining heart.

CHAPTER SEVEN
TRISTAN, AGE 20

One Year Later

IT WAS HIS first visit home since he'd left for university. Everything and nothing was the same.

Pater had more gray streaks in his long hair, or silver as Father lovingly called it. And Father was thinner than before, but still hardy enough, thank wolf-god. Hudson was spoiled but adorable, and Max was presenting early as an alpha, which Tristan had seen coming long ago.

Zekial was in the town now, working with the doctor there to learn new skills.

Pater said there was word that he'd developed a crush on an age mate, the son of a beta shopkeeper, but Zekie was always private about his feelings, and so none of them knew for sure.

The person most changed, though, was Tristan himself.

After two years in the city, Hud's Basin was too quiet for him to sleep. He tossed and turned in the bed that had once seemed plenty big and comfortable, but now felt narrow and hard. The house was cold, too, with frigid night air leaking in from the edges of his window and settling over him like a blanket. Once he'd adored cuddling up with his soft blankets, feeling the touch of cold air on his skin. He'd felt safe and sound and solid.

Now he was restless and uncomfortable and out of sorts.

Giving up on sleep, he stole from his room and down to the kitchen. As quietly as he could, he put on a kettle and lit the stove.

Perhaps hot tea would soothe him. While he was carefully adding the herbs Pater got from Fan, the blend of dried leaves in the tin marked "sleep", he tried to determine why he didn't seem to fit anymore. The bed, the house, and Hud's Basin itself felt like a pair of pants he'd outgrown.

"Trouble sleeping?"

His father's voice almost startled Tristan into dropping the newly filled teapot as he turned from the stove to the table.

"Ah, yes." Tristan shrugged. "Probably all that napping on the train. It's got my schedule confused."

"Likely," Father agreed.

"Go on back to bed. I'm all right."

Father tightened his robe around his middle and sat down at the table with a yawn. "How about I keep you company for a bit instead?"

"Of course." Tristan poured tea for his father, too, and they drank their first sips in silence.

"So, you saw him," Father said.

Tristan's stomach tightened. How did Father know? Tristan hadn't told anyone he was going to the prison to meet the man who'd made him. No one but Bek, and Bek would never tell a soul. His expression must have given his confusion away, because Father went on to clarify, "He sent a letter. The first one ever. I think your pater only read it because, when he saw it was from the prison, he assumed it was a notice of his death."

"Was Pater angry?" Tristan whispered.

Father shook his head.

"Disappointed, then?" That was so much worse.

Father considered that. "He was afraid. But I reminded him that you're a grown alpha now, fully capable of taking care of yourself and that no harm had come to you."

Tristan shivered, a cold sweat breaking over him. "I didn't want Pater to know. I just wanted to...meet him. For myself. To see what he's like. I needed to know."

"We all have to confront our demons. I imagine, after all the years of overhearing whispers and innuendos, of us warning you against the Monhundy family, your father had turned into a pretty big demon for you."

Tristan nodded. Leave it to Father to understand so completely. "He's just an old, sick man. Older than he is in years, you know? I thought he'd be big and brutal after the way Pater trembles whenever he comes up in conversation, and I know he used to be. But now he's shrunken and sickly. Cancer is what he said."

Father nodded and said nothing. He took a sip of his tea.

"What did his letter say?" Tristan grimaced, imagining his pater's reaction to it. "Was it terrible?"

"He said you'd grown into a fine young man, and he thanked Kerry for allowing you to visit."

Tristan felt the blood drain from his face.

"Oh, wolf-god."

"He took it better than you're imagining. Though he did cry."

Tristan buried his face in his hands. The idea of his stern, scolding, soft-but-hard pater crying was too horrible. And because of him. Again. "I know that I caused Pater a lot of pain—"

"It was just a visit to a dying man in jail," Father said. "It was a drop of bitterness in an ocean of joy. You have been a wonderful son. We're proud of you."

Tristan's throat ached. "I meant that I caused Pater pain by existing. By being Wilbet Monhundy's son."

Father whispered fiercely, "What did I tell you when you left for the city? You are *my* son."

"Father, please, I'm trying to explain why I went to see him."

Father rubbed a hand over his mouth, like he was holding back more words, and then nodded. "Go on. I'll let you talk."

"The city is different than I thought it would be," Tristan began. "The other alphas…they're all so proud of their lineage. They won't let me forget that I'm not a Heelies."

Father's jaw clenched, but he kept his word and let Tristan continue.

"And the longer I stayed in the city, the more I thought that maybe I don't *want* to be a Heelies…"

Father's eyes flickered with hurt.

"Not because I don't love the Heelies family, but because I love one of them *too* much."

Father's brows rose with interest, but he kept his mouth shut.

"It doesn't matter how *I* feel, though, because the man who has my heart is going to contract with the alpha heir to the Sabel fortune. But, I admit, Father, I thought that maybe if the Monhundy family estate were mine, the way it would have been if… Well, I admit I wondered if maybe I'd have a better chance with him." Tristan winced. "It was foolish. He barely even sees me. Not while Viro exists in the world."

"They're *Érosgápe*?"

Tristan shook his head. "No, but they may as well be. Riki believes Viro is his future."

"Riki," Father whispered. "Caleb's Riki."

Tristan felt his cheeks heat. "I know he's older than I am. Wolf-god, I know it's wrong for a lot of reasons. Like the fact that I'm Tristan Heelies, and he's Riki Heelies. Legally, he's my cousin—but he's not. You're my father in my heart," Tristan touched his chest, "but I was made from Monhundy flesh. Not yours."

Father's jaw moved again like he wanted to argue, but he just inclined his head.

"So, I went to see him. The man who made me. He wasn't what I'd expected from the hushed tales I'd overheard. I know he brutalized Pater, that he raped and hurt people." Tristan's eyes burned, and his throat hurt. "I don't like him. I don't admire him. But the danger is over, isn't it? I'm grown now, and I'm a good man. If I met his parents, if they accepted me as their grandson, and the estate came to me…" Tristan trailed off. His tea had grown cold. His toes ached, they were so frozen.

"If that happened?" Janus asked.

"I suppose I'd have a lot money to soothe my loneliness." Tristan smirked. "Because I know it won't buy me Riki's love. Viro Sabel has plenty of money, and Riki has a huge enough allowance of his own. It was foolish to think it'd matter."

"Desperate men do desperate things."

Tristan nodded, taking a sip of his tea. "Yes. But I don't regret knowing Riki. I could never regret that."

"I understand." Father sat quietly, a frown on his face. "What about the Monhundys, then?"

"I won't see him again. Prison is too miserable. He wasn't unkind to me, but I know what he did to Pater and to others. Once was enough."

"Good."

"I do plan to meet my grandparents. I reached out to them, but they were traveling. They asked for an 'audience'—their word—when they return from their trip to Cayo." Tristan reached out and took hold of his father's hand. "Please, don't think this means anything about you. I know you're my father. My heart knows it."

"So does mine."

Tristan said firmly, "I love you."

"I love you, too. You're my son. No matter where your flesh came from."

They gripped fingers, but finally, Tristan let go. He rubbed his forehead and sighed. "I didn't want Pater to know about all of this. I know how the memories still pain him. Though, I suppose if things go the way I hope, there will be no getting out of telling him."

"Explaining your sudden wealth would

be difficult, yes."

Tristan smirked. "I don't expect it will change me."

"Money changes all men." Father smiled knowingly. "But it doesn't have to change them for the worse."

"Will he forgive me?"

"Your pater loves you, Tristan. You are part of his heart cleaved from his body, like all of your brothers. He'll understand."

"Will he?"

"He is a smart man, a kind man."

"He hated them. My whole life, he feared they'd come for me. And now…I'm going to them…"

"Let me handle your pater. He'll understand. This is something you have to do. For many reasons."

"Thank you, Father," Tristan said, his throat tight and voice gruff. "I was afraid you'd be angry or think I didn't love you enough."

"I know you love me," Father said. "I'm

not worried about that. I have faith that our love and devotion to you has instilled an incorruptible sense of right and wrong. And if you get confused, if *they* work to confuse you, then I believe you'll come to me—to us—for help."

Tristan rose from the table and crossed to kneel at his father's feet. He pressed his face against Janus's chest and scented his warm, strong alpha smell, and then pressed a kiss to his cheek before rising. "Thank you, Father. For believing in me. For understanding."

Father rose, too, grabbing him into a hug. He kissed his cheek. "Go to bed soon, Tristan. Hudson will be up early to see what winter-fox brings."

TRISTAN STOOD FROZEN by his bedroom window, peering down toward Chewy's old den. He stared in disbelief as a wildcat family crept out of the woods—first the father cat, then the mother, and finally two small kittens. He watched, stunned, as the two small kittens were herded inside the old den by their brilliant-eyed mother. The father stood guardian outside, his proud head high, and his tail twitching in the air.

Surely he was dreaming.

But then again, winter-fox always did bring him the best gifts.

CHAPTER EIGHT

The next morning

"TRISTAN." MAX'S VOICE was soft but strangely urgent. "Tristan, wake up."

"Hmm?"

"Come downstairs," his little brother said in his gruff, newly deep tone. His dark hair hung down over his shoulders, long like their pater's, and still messy. "Hurry."

"Why?" Then he remembered. The holiday. The gifts. "Did winter-fox come for Hudson?"

"C'mon. Hurry. You'll see," Max said, and then rushed from the room, his pajamas covered by a green robe that had once been

Tristan's.

Tristan took the time to relieve his bladder, run a damp hand through his hair, and pull on a robe of his own. His was pink and blue paisley silk, purchased by his Uncle Caleb for his birthday. It was one of his favorite pieces of clothing, and he treasured it. Still, he was half-tempted to leave it behind in Hud's Basin for Max…

He started down the stairs and paused near the bottom. Voices drifted from the living room, all of them familiar, but not all of them belonging to his Hud's Basin family.

"More coffee, then?" Zekial asked, his timber deeper than ever, but his brashness recognizable anywhere.

"Yes, please."

Tristan's heart jolted, and he shot from the stairs down the hall, blood rushing wildly. Entering the living room, his eyes brushed over the decorated tree, knobby-kneed Hudson on the floor pushing the trains from the set winter-fox had put out the night before, Max standing by the fire with wide eyes, and his sweet Zekie hovering by the man on the couch.

Hudson pushed his trains around the track, his chugging noises huffing on his breath. When he looked up and saw Tristan frozen in the doorway, he cocked his dark head, grinned, and said, "Look what winter-fox brought you, Tristan. A friend." He turned to the man on the couch. "What are you called again?"

"Riki," Tristan breathed before rushing forward to kneel at the beautiful omega's feet. "Why are you here? What's happened?"

Riki's eyes were red and swollen, tear tracks were still evident on his cheeks, and when his gaze met Tristan's, his brittle composure broke. He leaned forward into Tristan's arms, his sobs rocking him wildly and his body trembling hard. "Viro…" he gritted out, and then he sobbed some more.

The boys shifted back and forth until Zekial ushered them from the room, with only a small grumble from Hudson about leaving his trains behind. However, the promise of Max letting him eat some of the sweet dough as he started on the feast for later in the day shut him up quickly.

"Talk to me," Tristan said when Riki had stopped crying. "Is everyone safe?" He didn't want to ask if anyone was dead. He didn't know what to ask at all. He'd never seen this proud man so undone, so lost and miserable. "Are all of your parents all right? What about Sam, Levi, Bek, and Ray?"

Riki sat back, wiped his eyes, and whispered, "My family's all right. But I had to go. I had to leave. I've lost him." His lips crumpled again. "Viro...I've lost him."

"He found his *Érosgápe*?"

Riki nodded, a sob bursting from him.

Tristan sat beside him on the couch, pulled him close, and wondered why it was that Riki had come to *him*. Of all the places to go in the world, of all the men to seek out, why Hud's Basin, and why him? He hadn't known Riki even thought of him as much of a friend. But it didn't matter. Riki was here now, with him, and he would do anything to stop his pain.

When Riki stopped crying again, Tristan murmured, "Do you believe in winter-fox?"

Riki snorted softly but said nothing, turning his tear-wet face against Tristan's hot neck. Tristan stroked his fingers through Riki's soft curls, his heart galloping with concern and shock that the man he adored was clinging to him. "I believe in him," Tristan whispered. "He brought me a wildcat once."

"You told me."

"I saw my wildcat last night. Outside near his old den. With his mate and his young."

Riki wiped at his wet cheeks, his nose red and his eyes iridescent with grief. "Oh?"

"And this morning, I woke to find you here."

"Winter-fox didn't bring me. Your

brother did."

"Winter-fox brought my brother, though. Not last night, but the night he was born."

"Tristan…" Riki said his name like a plea. "I don't understand. You're confusing me."

"I'm sorry." Tristan pushed a stray curl from Riki's forehead. "Why did you come here, Riki? To Hud's Basin? To me?"

"I don't know," Riki said softly. "I had to go somewhere. So, I took the train and got off at Blumzound because I remembered that's where you said you went to come home."

"And how did you find Zekial?"

"It was late in the afternoon when I got off the train, and I didn't know how to get to Hud's Basin. I went into a pastry shop, thinking a tart might help me feel better. But instead, I started to cry, and the shopkeeper panicked."

"Bill?"

"Yes, that's his name. His son Uli was there with Zekial." Riki sounded far away as if he were talking from the bottom of a lake.

"Ah, yes." Tristan knew Zekial stayed with Bill's family while working with the doctor in town.

"It was late in the day, though, and I cried a long time. I just couldn't seem to stop."

"It's all right."

"After I calmed down it was already night, and Zekial offered to drive me up the mountain to you in the morning. I slept on Bill's couch." Riki flushed even more pink than his tears had already left him. "Except I couldn't sleep. I think my crying bothered your brother because sometime before sun-up he came out of his room and said we should go."

"Zekial is tender-hearted," Tristan said.

"Like you," Riki murmured.

Two sets of heavy footsteps sounded on the stairs, and Tristan rushed to shut the door to the living room so that they wouldn't be interrupted by his father or pater. When he returned to Riki, he found that Riki looked even more haunted.

"Let me get that coffee Zekie promised you," Tristan whispered.

Riki grabbed his arm. "Just sit with me. I don't want to be alone right now. Not even for a minute."

Tristan did as he was asked. Voices came from the kitchen, muffled through the closed door, individual phrases and words indecipherable. No one disturbed them. No one even knocked.

"Today is the Feast of Winter's Heart," Tristan offered. "We have our traditional sweets."

Riki nodded and then turned to Tristan urgently. "Do you remember last year? How we sat together to hear the bells?"

Tristan nodded.

"I almost kissed you then."

Tristan's head swam. "Oh? I..." he

cleared his throat. "I almost kissed you, too."

"But I had promised my heart to Viro."

Tristan's pulse thundered. "Yes."

"He never really wanted it."

"Didn't he?"

Riki shook his head and wiped at his eyes, and his voice shook as he asked, "Do you want it, Tristan?"

"Your heart?"

Riki nodded, his face crumpling. "If I gave it to you? Would you want it?"

Tristan pulled Riki close and tucked his head beneath his chin, breathing in the delicious honey-sweetness of his hair. Trembling, he said, "When I was very young, I thought that *Érosgápe* traded hearts. That their hearts came out of their chests and switched bodies."

Riki held very still.

"I don't know how I thought it happened. Magic, I guess. But I believed that."

Riki's heart beat so hard and fast that Tristan could feel it shaking his lithe body.

"Any man would be lucky to have your heart, Riki," Tristan whispered. "But I don't think you're really ready to give it to anyone yet."

"But if I were ready? Would you even want it?"

"I wouldn't just take it. I'd trade with you," Tristan whispered. "I'd give you my heart, too."

Riki shook quietly in Tristan's arms, but neither said much more. The morning sun slipped higher in the sky, and finally, there came a timid knock. Pater opened the door slightly and said, "There's coffee and breakfast…"

Riki sat up and straightened his clothes, wiped his face, and cleared his throat. He nodded at Tristan.

"You're sure?" Tristan whispered.

"Yes," Riki said, rising, though he shook like a leaf. "I can't be rude to your family."

"They'd understand."

Still, Riki moved toward the door, his

strides graceful and strong. So, Tristan followed.

Once they were at the kitchen table, Tristan introduced everyone to Riki. Then he sat back and watched as his whole family behaved as if Riki wasn't a blotchy, miserable mess. They passed the butter and jam, the syrup, and the pot of coffee, discussing the plans for the feast that afternoon.

Tristan's eyes continually returned to Riki—so elegant even in his distress—softly thanking Pater for the food and complimenting Max on his cooking. His heart felt rended in half—as if part of himself now sat across the table, trying hard to move on from the grief of a future lost, if only long enough to eat a civil breakfast.

Oh, Riki.

He had so many questions—who was the *Érosgápe* Viro had found? Where had Viro discovered him? What was Riki's plan for the future now? Why had he come to Tristan in Hud's Basin? Had he meant it when he asked if Tristan wanted his heart?

But he held his tongue and trusted in the unfolding of the uncertain future. There wasn't much else he could do.

His grandpater and pater had always adapted to whatever circumstances came their way, and so Tristan would, too. He might be a Monhundy by flesh, and perhaps soon he'd have their wealth as well, but he was his pater's son, and that meant he could be patient. Very patient.

"Do you mind if I stay here a while?" Riki asked after the feast was over.

They were in the living room together having seen Zekie off back to Bloundzound. Max had gone up to his room to nap, exhausted after making most of the meal since Tristan had been too busy with Riki to help, and Hudson was asleep on Father's lap, his thumb in his mouth.

The fire roared, and the moment of silence following Riki's question was filled with the crackle of the firewood.

"It's a boarding house," Father said with a smile and a glance toward Tristan. "There's plenty of room."

"But you'll need to let your family know where you are," Pater said. "They don't know, do they?"

Riki shook his head, his eyes falling to where his fingers knitted together in his lap.

"They'll be worried."

Riki nodded this time, keeping his silence. Tristan reached out and squeezed his hands. His heart trembled when Riki took hold of his fingers and clung to them.

Father caught Tristan's eye. Obviously, they'd be talking about this eventually, but not this night.

"Perhaps when Tristan goes back after the winter break, you can ride to the city together," Pater said, his knitting needles clacking away. It was soothing to Tristan, familiar, and brought back memories of him falling asleep by the fire to the sound.

"I'm not going back," Riki said faintly.

"Never?" Tristan asked, and Pater looked up sharply from his knitting. Father tilted his head and met Tristan's eyes again.

"Never," Riki said with a fiery kind of exhaustion.

Tristan decided then and there he wouldn't go back to the city without Riki either. Wherever Riki went, so long as he agreed to have Tristan by his side, he'd go, too. As for his 'audience' with the Munhundys, they could take the train to Bloundzound to meet *him*. He didn't need to see their mansion in the city again or endure any crass attempts to lure him into their world with stories of what might have been. He'd be just as happy to meet them from the comfort of his hometown. So long as Riki was in Hud's Basin, Tristan wasn't leaving.

The rest of the day passed in a strange mash of family and Riki. That night, as the moon rose above the trees and the sweets from the feast rested heavy in their stomachs, Tristan held Riki's hand and walked him down toward Chewy's den. There they stood and watched as Chewy's mate paced the boundary between the forest and the lawn.

Riki clenched Tristan's hand in fear as the bushes rustled, and then Chewy himself broke free of them. He'd grown so large and strong in the years since Tristan had seen him.

"How old do wildcats live to be?" Riki murmured. "Are you sure he's the same one from your childhood."

"If they don't get caught in a trap or shot, they can live to be twenty or so," Tristan whispered. "And, yeah, I'd recognize him anywhere." His heart soared as the cat caught his eye and held it. Dangerous. There was no doubt about it. And yet Tristan didn't move away, and Riki stood bravely at his side, the two of them hand-in-hand.

Chewy strolled forward, a brown rabbit in his sharp teeth.

A rabbit which he dropped at Tristan's feet.

He then nuzzled against Tristan's thigh.

"Holy wolf-god," Riki breathed, holding very still. Tristan was sure he could feel the rush of Riki's pulse in his palm pressed so firmly against his own.

Chewy sized Riki up for a long moment, and Tristan's heart also pounded. Even after all these years, he trusted Chewy, and yet…

Chewy broke away from watching Riki to nuzzle Tristan's hand. Scratching lightly behind his ears, Tristan laughed softly as Chewy began to purr and rub against Tristan's legs, and then over to Riki's legs, too.

Riki gasped softly.

"He's marking us with his scent," Tristan whispered. "He's telling his mate that we're safe, that we're his, too."

Riki clenched his hand harder.

Then Chewy let loose a sound that drew his mate away from the boundary of the woods. She prowled forward with her small kittens right behind her.

"Oh wolf-god," Riki cursed again.

Chewy paraded proudly between his mate, his kittens, and Tristan.

"He's showing you his family," Riki whispered.

"Look at your family, Chewy," Tristan said. "They're wonderful."

Chewy nuzzled Tristan's hand once more and then herded his mate and kittens into the old den before bounding off into the woods again. The brown rabbit still lay at Tristan's feet. He didn't let go of Riki's hand as he bent to pick it up.

"What will you do with it?"

"Stew," Tristan said.

Riki huffed, and it was almost a laugh, almost as beautiful as the night of the bells. "That's the second most mountain-folk thing I've ever heard you say."

"Stick around, and you'll hear more."

Riki's elegant black coat caught the new snowflakes as they began to fall, standing out stark and white. "All right," he agreed. "I will."

Tristan's heart almost broke with the strength of his emotions.

"Thank you," Riki said, turning to Tristan with a sad smile on his lips. "For being the kind of man I could run to after I fell apart. I didn't even know I saw you like that until I needed someone, and I thought of you."

"Thank you for letting me be that man," Tristan said, and he brushed snow from Riki's cheekbone. He wanted to say so much more, but the time wasn't right. But he could be patient. Eventually, the day would come.

Just then, the mama cat and kittens again emerged from the den, and Tristan thought it would be best to get back into the house. Without Chewy around, he wasn't sure of her. Mama cats could be dangerous.

"Have I told you winter-fox brings me the best gifts?"

Riki squeezed his hand and nodded. Tristan fought the urge to tip Riki's chin up and kiss his lips. Instead, he settled for simply nodding toward the house, away from where the kittens wrestled. "We should go in," he said.

"Yes," Riki agreed, but they continued to stand still and watch the kittens play as snow drifted down around them. Like magic.

Look what winter-fox has brought me, Tristan thought, looking between the wildcat den, the mama cat, the kittens, the rabbit in his fist, and Riki's awed face. *What should I call it?*

He supposed he'd have to call it hope.

THE END

Heat of Love Series

"If you're an omegaverse fan, Leta Blake needs to be at the top of your autobuy list. I'm very picky about omegaverse romances, but everything about this series is impeccable—world-building, characterization, complex plots, and incredible sensual tension. Don't miss this one!"

—Annabeth Albert, author of Frozen Hearts series.

SLOW HEAT
- Series Starter
- Age Difference
- Younger Alpha/Older Omega
- Slow Burn
- Heat & Knotting

"Leta Blake is a literary force. Her rich and compelling characters and her dynamic world building, coupled with her skill as a story teller create a magical, one of a kind experience for the reader. The Heat of Love series is the best in its genre."

—EM Denning, author of Upstate Education series

ALPHA HEAT

- Age Difference
- Forbidden Love
- Two Alphas
- Damaged Heroes

"Leta Blake has created complex characters in challenging situations that will break your heart. This books handles some very heavy topics without going truly dark. I highly recommend the entire series!"

—DJ Jamison, author of Surprise Groom

BITTER HEAT

- Hurt/Comfort

- Pregnant Hero
- Forbidden Love
- Heat & Knotting

"Leta Blake has crafted an astonishing story of redemption and the peace that can only be found when you open yourself up to unexpected circumstance. Bitter Heat is a testament to the power of fate and the many different facets of love."

—Kate Hawthorne, author of Giving Consent series

SLOW BIRTH
- Vale & Jason from Slow Heat
- Dramatic Heat & Knotting
- Pregnant Hero
- Pregnancy Sex

read as an addition to the *Heat of Love* series, preferably after reading *Slow Heat*, *Alpha Heat*, and *Slow Birth*. But if you should happen to read it out of order, you can find the rest of the books in the series on Amazon and in Kindle Unlimited.

A Heat of Love bonus prequel novella by Leta Blake

WHITE HEAT

Forbidden love conquers all.

Sian Maxima, the heir to a great lineage, yearns to marry his childhood sweetheart, Avila Rossi. But their love is outlawed. After a secret, desperate tryst is discovered, Avila alone will be punished for their transgressions.

Only Sian can save him.

White Heat is a standalone prequel to Leta Blake's ***Heat of Love*** universe. It's set against a faux-historical backdrop and contains tropes such as mpreg, knotting, and heats.

HEAT FOR SALE
Heat can be sold but love is earned.

In a world where omegas sell their heats for profit, Adrien is a university student in need of funding. With no family to fall back on, he reluctantly allows the university's matcher to offer his virgin heat for auction online. Anxious, but aware this is the reality of life for all omegas, Adrien hopes whoever wins his heat will be kind.

Heath—a wealthy, older alpha—is rocked by the young man's resemblance to his dead lover, Nathan. When Heath discovers Adrien is Nathan's lost son from his first heat years before they met, he becomes obsessed with the idea of reclaiming a piece of Nathan.

Heath buys Adrien's heat with only one motivation: to impregnate Adrien, claim the child, and move on. But their undeniable passion shocks him. Adrien doesn't know what to make of the handsome, mysterious stranger he's pledged his body to, but he's soon swept away in the heat of the moment and surrenders to Heath entirely.

Once Adrien is pregnant, Heath secrets him away to his immense and secluded home. As the birth draws near, Heath grows to love Adrien for the man he is, not just for his connection to Nathan. Unaware of Heath's past with his omega parent and coming to depend on him heart and soul, Adrien begins to fall as well.

But as their love blossoms, Nathan's shadow looms. Can Heath keep his new love and the child they've made together once Adrien discovers his secrets?

Heat for Sale is a stand-alone m/m erotic romance by Leta Blake, writing as Blake Moreno. Infused with a du Maurier *Rebecca*-style secret, it features a well-realized omegaverse, an age-gap, dominance and submission, heats, knotting, and scorching hot scenes.

BULLY FOR SALE

Bullied and outcast, Ezer has seen firsthand the cruelties of the world. He knows what's expected from his kind—timid compliance to his "betters." But Ezer isn't one to conform to the role society has forced upon him.

Despite his defiant nature, Ezer must partner with a man of his father's choosing, one his father promises will love and care for him for the rest of his life.

After the contract is signed, Ezer is horrified to discover his partner is Ned, a member of the pack of bullies who have made his life so distressing. Ezer's determined to hate Ned, but he can't help the way he reacts to his touch.

Ned is young, privileged, and hopelessly in love with Ezer. Unfortunately, his pack of so-called "friends" have targeted Ezer for torment. Ned has a lot of regrets, but none greater than his role in Ezer's misery. When Ned's offered the contract of a lifetime, he sees it as the only way to prove he's worthy of Ezer's love.

Too bad Ezer is just as determined not to fall for his bully.

OMEGA MINE: SEARCH FOR A SOUL MATE

Can an Alpha find his dream Omega on reality TV?

Alpha Hank Morrow is a police officer and Alpha bear shifter who has never found the right Omega. Without the steadying influence of a bond with his Omega, Hank's powerful Alpha senses are beginning to overwhelm and endanger not only him, but his fellow police officers and the entire city of White Edge. The chief of police and the governor sign Hank up for a reality TV show to help unmatched Alphas find their dream Omega.

Omega Mine: Search for a Soulmate certainly isn't Hank's idea of a great plan, but he's not given a choice. Now he's off to a tropical island to meet over one hundred potential Omegas in a televised version of hell.

Or is it?

Evan Vaughn is an unmatched Omega. He and Hank have actually met once before at an Alpha-Omega mixer, but apparently he didn't make much of an impression at the time. Will that change on the set of *Omega Mine*? And can anything real come out of a reality TV dating show? Hank and Evan are about to find out...

***The Bachelor* meets Alpha-Omega romance!**

This book is nearly 40,000 words of an oblivious bear shifter finally meeting his soul bonded match and a happy ending you'll love! Warning: There is no mfm in this book. There is no ménage in this book. There is no cheating in this book. There is an attraction to someone that is not the other MC but it does not come to fruition.

FLIGHT

There's no greater mystery in the kingdom than where Prince Mateo's sisters disappear to each night. The king is determined to discover where they go and issues a challenge to all the nobles to help him learn their secret. Hoping to protect them, Mateo hides beneath a magic cloak and follows his sisters to an enchanted world of fairies and lusty delights.

Ópalo has waited years to finally meet his human lover. Fairies are bound by fate, and Ópalo is eager to embrace his, and plans a future with Mateo. But while Mateo soon succumbs to the pleasures of the flesh, he refuses to surrender his heart so easily.

As their worlds collide, Ópalo has to risk everything to win his man forever.

Gay Romance Newsletter

Leta's newsletter will keep you up to date on her latest releases and news from the world of M/M romance. Join the mailing list today and you're automatically entered into future giveaways.

Leta Blake on Patreon

Become part of Leta Blake's Patreon community in order to access exclusive content, deleted scenes, extras, bonus stories, rewards, prizes, interviews, and more. www.patreon.com/letablake

Other Books by Leta Blake

Contemporary

Will & Patrick Wake Up Married
Will & Patrick's Endless Honeymoon
Cowboy Seeks Husband
The Difference Between
Bring on Forever
Stay Lucky

Sports

The River Leith

The Training Season Series
Training Season
Training Complex

Musicians

Smoky Mountain Dreams
Vespertine

New Adult

Punching the V-Card

'90s Coming of Age Series
Pictures of You
You Are Not Me
Only You

Winter Holidays

North's Pole

The Mr. Christmas Series
Mr. Frosty Pants
Mr. Naughty List
Mr. Jingle Bells

A Boy for All Seasons
My December Daddy

Fantasy

Any Given Lifetime

Reimagined Fairy Tales

Flight
Levity

Paranormal & Shifters

Angel Undone
Omega Mine

Horror

Raise Up Heart

Omegaverse

Heat of Love Series
White Heat
Slow Heat
Alpha Heat
Slow Birth
Bitter Heat

For Sale Series

Heat for Sale
Bully for Sale

Audiobooks
letablake.com/audiobooks

Discover more about the author online

Leta Blake
letablake.com

About the Author

Author of the bestselling book *Smoky Mountain Dreams* and fan favorites like *Training Season*, *Will & Patrick Wake Up Married*, and *Slow Heat*, Leta Blake has been captivating M/M Romance readers for over a decade. Whether writing contemporary romance or fantasy, she puts her psychology background to use creating complex characters and love stories that feel real. At home in the Southern U.S., Leta works hard at achieving balance between her writing and her family life.